Ozzie and the ART CONTEST

Words and Pictures
by Dana Sullivan

It was art time...

and Ozzie was painting his masterpiece.

His teacher, Miss Cattywhompus, announced, "The big art contest is coming up next week."

"Remember to read the instructions very carefully and bring me your best pictures on Monday."

On the way home Ozzie glanced at the instructions.

"She wants us to draw a goat. I'm an **EXPERT** on goats!

I'm going to win this contest."

All weekend Ozzie worked on his picture.

His neighbor Billy posed for him.

"Not baaaaaad," bleated Billy.
"This picture will take first prize!"

On Monday the class gave their pictures to Miss Cattywhompus.

"What marvelous artwork," she said.
"The winners will be on the board tomorrow."

Ozzie was so excited he could hardly sleep that night.

The next day everyone crowded around the bulletin board to see who had won the contest.

Ozzie pushed to the front, but he couldn't find his picture anywhere. He saw the winners. They were okay, but they weren't his.

Then he noticed another row of pictures under the words "Honorable Mention."

"Oh no!" thought Ozzie. "That's not where my picture should be. I'm an **EXPERT** on goats. I was supposed to win!"

That afternoon they had a big party. The class ate
cake and wore silly hats. Everybody had fun.

Everybody except Ozzie.

Miss Cattywhompus went to his desk.

"Ozzie, are you okay? You always bark the loudest when we have a party."

Ozzie almost started crying.

"I worked really hard on my goat picture," he said. "I was sure I would win. But all I got was Honorable Mention."

"Oh, Ozzie," said Miss Cattywhompus,
"winning isn't the only reason to do things.

Especially when it's something you really like to do."

"Besides, Honorable Mention is pretty good, since you drew a picture of a **Goat**."

"A **BOAT**!" barked Ozzie. "I was supposed to draw a **boat**?"

"Yes, Ozzie. You are a very good artist, but you need to pay more attention to your reading."

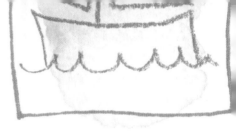

Suddenly Ozzie felt a lot better.

He went back to the bulletin board and, sure enough, all the winners were pictures of boats.

HONORABLE M

That gave Ozzie an idea.

"Look, everybody!"
he shouted.

To my sweet Vicki
and Max, the real-life inspiration
for Ozzie.

Dana Sullivan

Sleeping Bear Press

315 E. Eisenhower Parkway, Ste. 200
Ann Arbor, MI 48108
www.sleepingbearpress.com

Printed and bound in the United States.

10 9 8 7 6 5 4 3 2 1

Library of Congress Cataloging-in-Publication Data

Sullivan, Dana, 1958-
Ozzie and the art contest / by Dana Sullivan.
pages cm
Summary: Ozzie the dog loves to draw and when his kindergarten teacher announces
an art contest, he is sure he will win but he fails to follow directions, loses the contest,
and is sad until Miss Cattywhompus reminds him that art is not about winning.
ISBN 978-1-58536-820-4
[1. Drawing—Fiction. 2. Contests—Fiction. 3. Schools—Fiction.
4. Dogs—Fiction. 5. Animals—Fiction.] I. Title.
PZ7.S951370zz 2013
[E]—dc23
2013004098

Acknowledgments
Thanks to Tina Hoggatt for the push,
Peggy King Anderson for the cheerleading,
and Secret Agent Anna Olswanger for working
me like a dog until the story was just right. And
then working me some more, just for fun. Ozzie
is an Australian/French Ultramarine Blue Heeler
and loves watercolor and black ink.